MERLIN AND THE MAKING OF THE KING

MERLIN AND THE MAKING OF THE KING

RETOLD BY

MARGARET hodges

from Sir Thomas Malory's
Le Morte d'Arthur

ILLUSTRATED BY

TRINA SCHART hyMAN

HOLIDAY HOUSE / NEW YORK

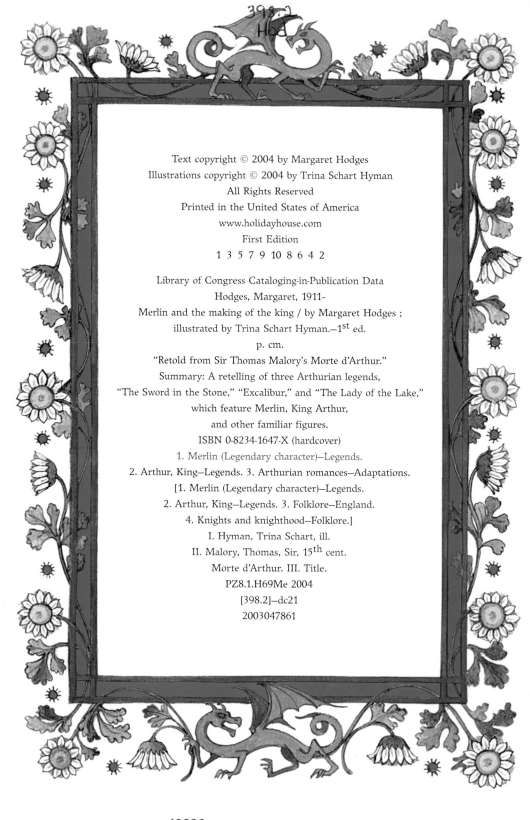

Library of Congress Cataloging-in-Publication Data
Hodges, Margaret, 1911–
Merlin and the making of the king / by Margaret Hodges ;
illustrated by Trina Schart Hyman.—1st ed.
p. cm.
"Retold from Sir Thomas Malory's Morte d'Arthur."
Summary: A retelling of three Arthurian legends,
"The Sword in the Stone," "Excalibur," and "The Lady of the Lake,"
which feature Merlin, King Arthur,
and other familiar figures.
ISBN 0-8234-1647-X (hardcover)
1. Merlin (Legendary character)—Legends.
2. Arthur, King—Legends. 3. Arthurian romances—Adaptations.
[1. Merlin (Legendary character)—Legends.
2. Arthur, King—Legends. 3. Folklore—England.
4. Knights and knighthood—Folklore.]
I. Hyman, Trina Schart, ill.
II. Malory, Thomas, Sir, 15th cent.
Morte d'Arthur. III. Title.
PZ8.1.H69Me 2004
[398.2]—dc21
2003047861

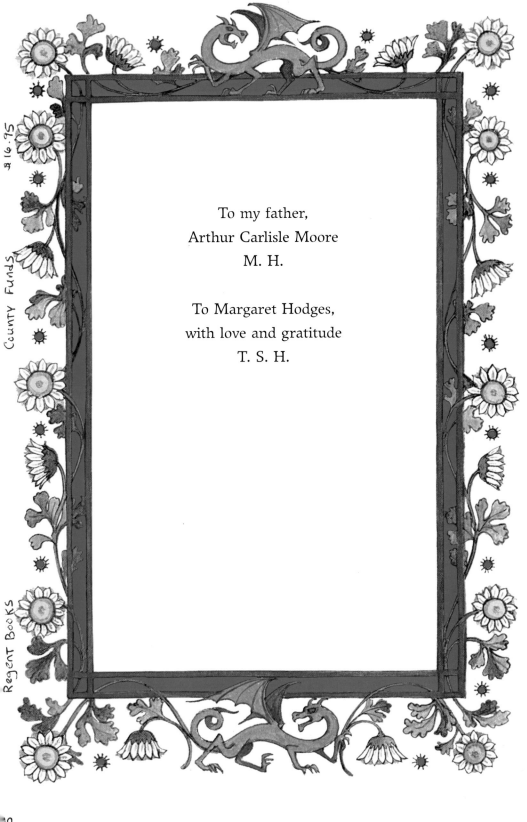

To my father,
Arthur Carlisle Moore
M. H.

To Margaret Hodges,
with love and gratitude
T. S. H.

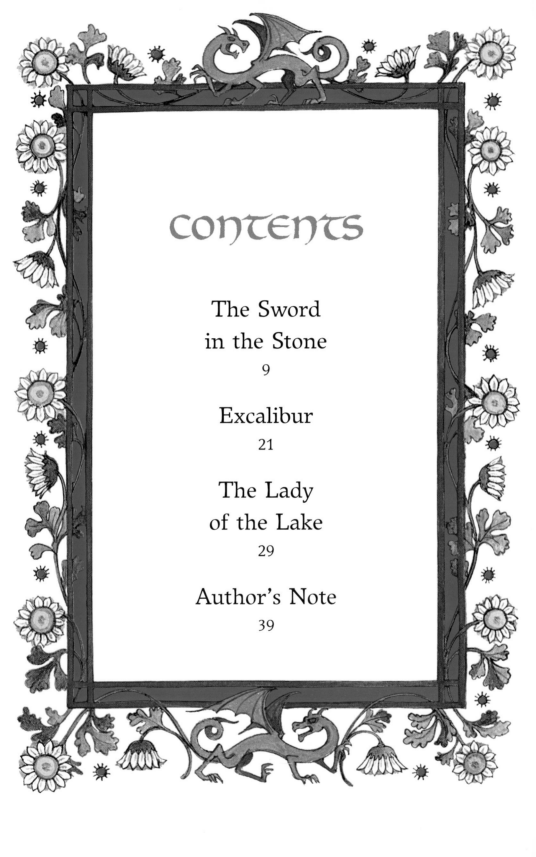

CONTENTS

THE SWORD
IN THE
STONE

N THE DAYS BEFORE Arthur was born, Merlin the magician hid himself in a cave that faced the western sea. No one ever saw Merlin if he did not wish to be seen, and no one knew that he was at work in his cave, making a great round table. Above the cave towered a castle called Tintagel, where the Duke of Cornwall lived with his beautiful wife, Igraine. All day long the duke's armed knights, soldiers, and servants were climbing up or down past the

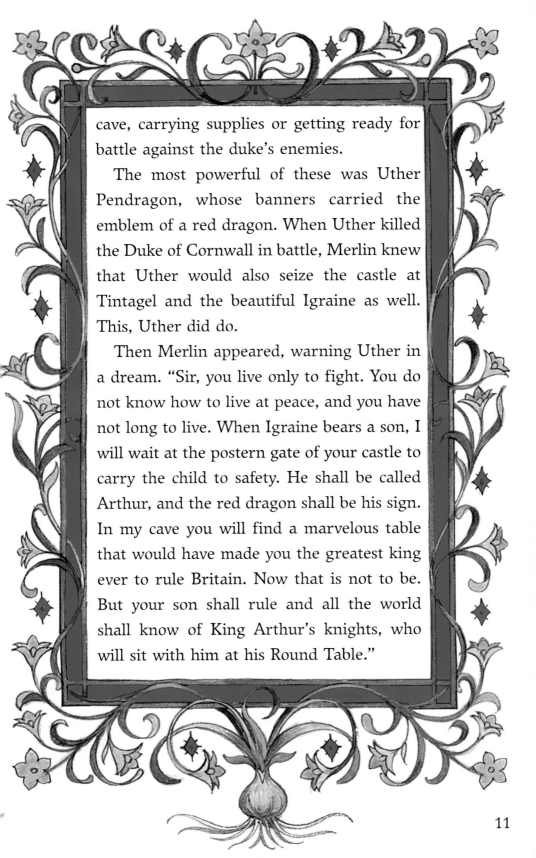

cave, carrying supplies or getting ready for battle against the duke's enemies.

The most powerful of these was Uther Pendragon, whose banners carried the emblem of a red dragon. When Uther killed the Duke of Cornwall in battle, Merlin knew that Uther would also seize the castle at Tintagel and the beautiful Igraine as well. This, Uther did do.

Then Merlin appeared, warning Uther in a dream. "Sir, you live only to fight. You do not know how to live at peace, and you have not long to live. When Igraine bears a son, I will wait at the postern gate of your castle to carry the child to safety. He shall be called Arthur, and the red dragon shall be his sign. In my cave you will find a marvelous table that would have made you the greatest king ever to rule Britain. Now that is not to be. But your son shall rule and all the world shall know of King Arthur's knights, who will sit with him at his Round Table."

Uther believed Merlin's words. When Igraine's baby was born, she wrapped him in cloth of gold and carried him by night to the postern gate. There with tears she gave him to Merlin, who covered him with his cloak and disappeared. Uther found the great table in Merlin's cave and gave it for safekeeping to a faithful friend and ally.

Not long afterward Uther died, as Merlin had foreseen. But Arthur was safe. Merlin had taken him to the house of a good man, Sir Ector, whose wife nursed the baby as if

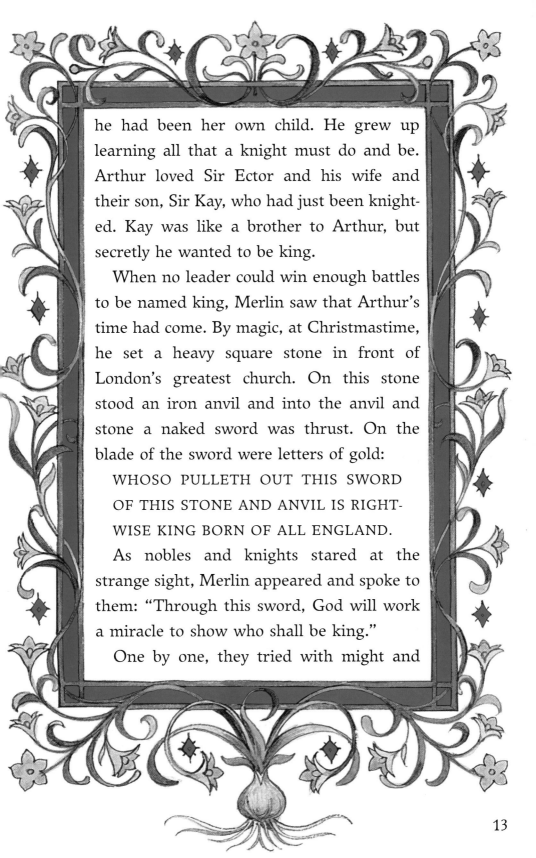

he had been her own child. He grew up learning all that a knight must do and be. Arthur loved Sir Ector and his wife and their son, Sir Kay, who had just been knighted. Kay was like a brother to Arthur, but secretly he wanted to be king.

When no leader could win enough battles to be named king, Merlin saw that Arthur's time had come. By magic, at Christmastime, he set a heavy square stone in front of London's greatest church. On this stone stood an iron anvil and into the anvil and stone a naked sword was thrust. On the blade of the sword were letters of gold:

WHOSO PULLETH OUT THIS SWORD OF THIS STONE AND ANVIL IS RIGHT-WISE KING BORN OF ALL ENGLAND.

As nobles and knights stared at the strange sight, Merlin appeared and spoke to them: "Through this sword, God will work a miracle to show who shall be king."

One by one, they tried with might and

main, but none could move the sword even a hairsbreadth.

"Have a tournament until a sign comes from heaven," said Merlin, and all agreed.

"But I forgot my sword," said Kay. "Arthur, go to my father's lodging and bring me a sword."

Arthur rode off willingly, but found the house locked and empty. Then he remembered the sword in the stone. He rode back to the churchyard. Everyone had gone to the tournament, and he found the sword untouched. He did not see Merlin standing in the shadows. Lightly Arthur took the sword by the hilt and smoothly he pulled it out of the stone. Then he found Sir Kay and said, "Here is a sword for you."

Amazed, Kay took it. He galloped off to his father and cried, "I have the sword of the stone! I must be king!"

But Sir Ector said, "Tell me on your oath, how did you get the sword?"

Kay was ashamed. "Arthur brought it to me," he said.

Sir Ector fell to his knees before Arthur, saying, "Now I know that Merlin spoke the truth when he brought you to my house as a baby. You are the son of Uther Pendragon, and you are the rightful king."

Then in the sight of all the great lords, Arthur thrust the sword into the stone and pulled it out easily. And though he alone could succeed in the marvelous feat, the lords

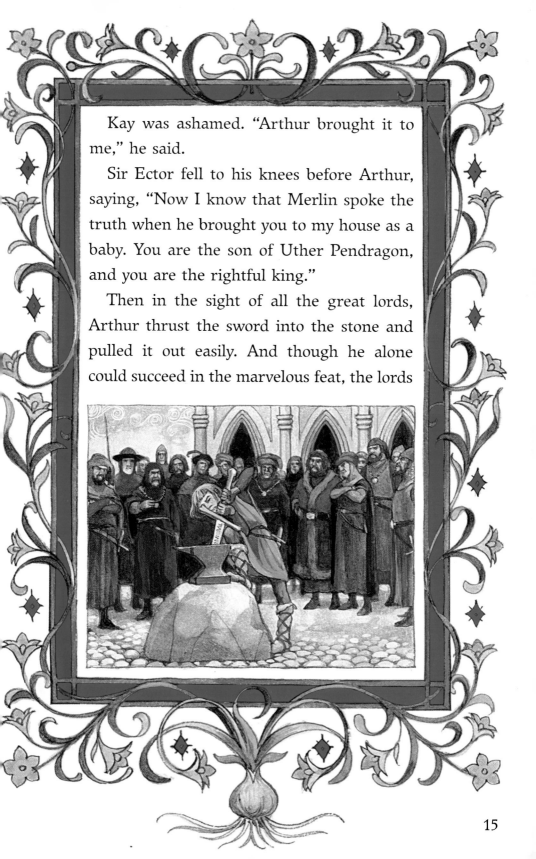

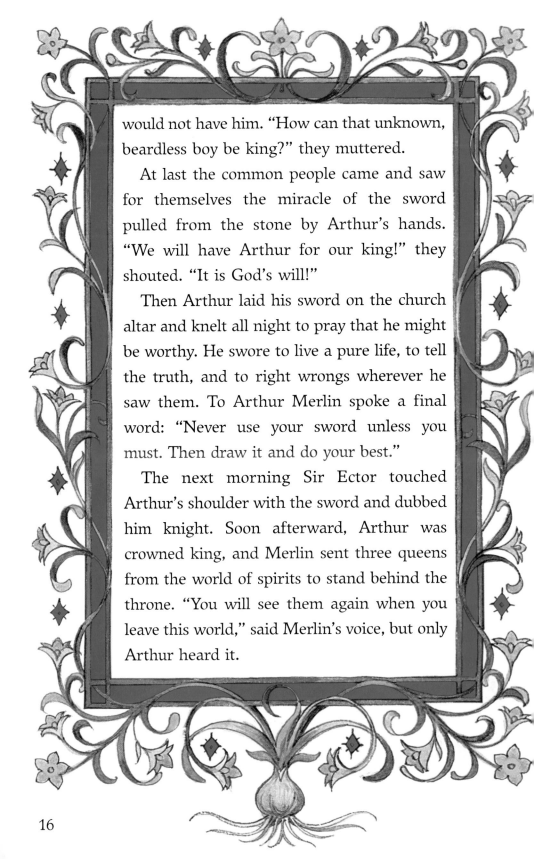

would not have him. "How can that unknown, beardless boy be king?" they muttered.

At last the common people came and saw for themselves the miracle of the sword pulled from the stone by Arthur's hands. "We will have Arthur for our king!" they shouted. "It is God's will!"

Then Arthur laid his sword on the church altar and knelt all night to pray that he might be worthy. He swore to live a pure life, to tell the truth, and to right wrongs wherever he saw them. To Arthur Merlin spoke a final word: "Never use your sword unless you must. Then draw it and do your best."

The next morning Sir Ector touched Arthur's shoulder with the sword and dubbed him knight. Soon afterward, Arthur was crowned king, and Merlin sent three queens from the world of spirits to stand behind the throne. "You will see them again when you leave this world," said Merlin's voice, but only Arthur heard it.

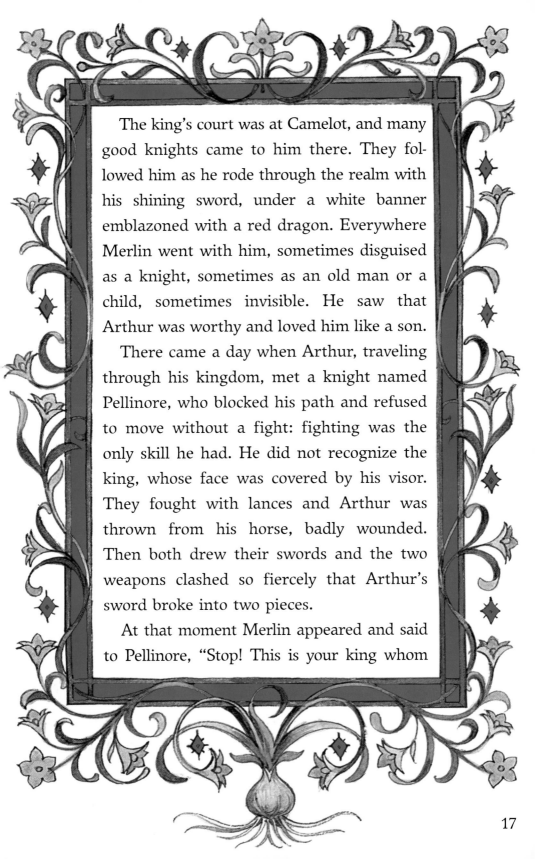

The king's court was at Camelot, and many good knights came to him there. They followed him as he rode through the realm with his shining sword, under a white banner emblazoned with a red dragon. Everywhere Merlin went with him, sometimes disguised as a knight, sometimes as an old man or a child, sometimes invisible. He saw that Arthur was worthy and loved him like a son.

There came a day when Arthur, traveling through his kingdom, met a knight named Pellinore, who blocked his path and refused to move without a fight: fighting was the only skill he had. He did not recognize the king, whose face was covered by his visor. They fought with lances and Arthur was thrown from his horse, badly wounded. Then both drew their swords and the two weapons clashed so fiercely that Arthur's sword broke into two pieces.

At that moment Merlin appeared and said to Pellinore, "Stop! This is your king whom

you are about to kill." Then he put Pellinore under a spell so that he fell into a deep sleep while Merlin rode away with Arthur to the cave of a hermit, who tended the king's wounds and saved his life.

Arthur wanted to return to Camelot. "But I have no sword," he said to Merlin.

"You shall have a better sword," said Merlin. "Come with me."

As they rode together, they came upon a hidden lake near the western sea. The waves sparkled in the sunlight, and by the shore near an ancient chapel lay a little boat. Then an arm rose from the middle of the lake, clothed in shining white, the hand grasping a sword with a richly jeweled hilt and scabbard.

A lovely young girl came toward them over the water, dressed in flowing green, and Merlin said, "That is Vivien, the Lady of the Lake, who lives in an enchanted palace deep under the water. The sword is hers."

The lady spoke to Arthur. "Go into yonder

boat with Merlin and row out to the sword. I give it and its scabbard to you."

Arthur and Merlin did as the lady commanded. Arthur took the sword and scabbard in both hands and the shining arm disappeared.

"The sword is called Excalibur," said Merlin. "It will never fail you as long as you use it in a good cause, not for your own glory. But the scabbard is better. It will protect you from loss of blood if you are wounded."

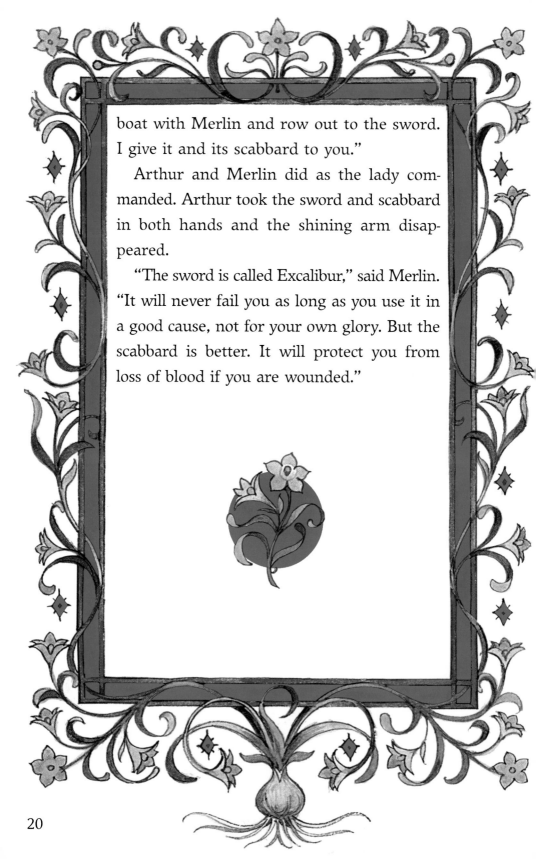

EXCALIBUR

ITH EXCALIBUR IN HIS HANDS, Arthur's power was great. Now it was time for him to marry and bring a queen to Camelot. He chose Guinevere, in Arthur's eyes the most beautiful of all the ladies.

"I cannot choose for you," Merlin warned him, "but I can tell you that this lady will bring you grief."

Arthur paid no heed to Merlin's words, and Guinevere's father gladly gave her in marriage

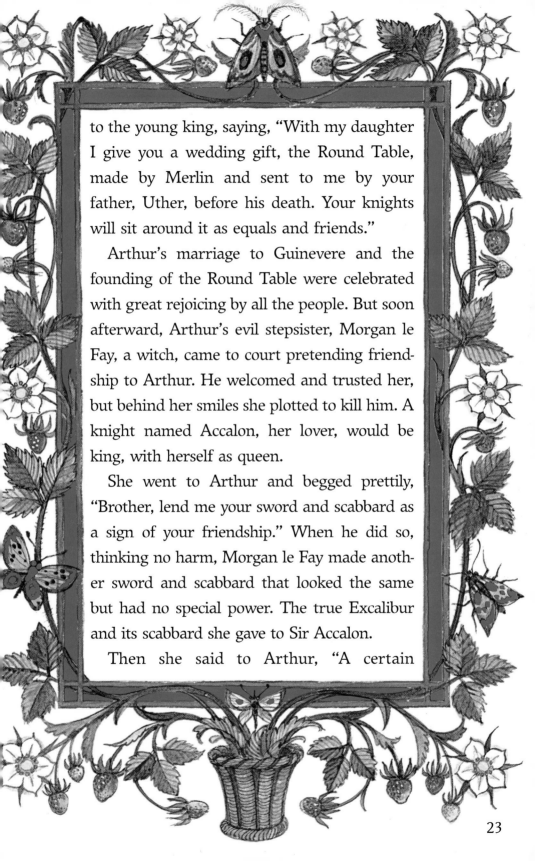

to the young king, saying, "With my daughter I give you a wedding gift, the Round Table, made by Merlin and sent to me by your father, Uther, before his death. Your knights will sit around it as equals and friends."

Arthur's marriage to Guinevere and the founding of the Round Table were celebrated with great rejoicing by all the people. But soon afterward, Arthur's evil stepsister, Morgan le Fay, a witch, came to court pretending friendship to Arthur. He welcomed and trusted her, but behind her smiles she plotted to kill him. A knight named Accalon, her lover, would be king, with herself as queen.

She went to Arthur and begged prettily, "Brother, lend me your sword and scabbard as a sign of your friendship." When he did so, thinking no harm, Morgan le Fay made another sword and scabbard that looked the same but had no special power. The true Excalibur and its scabbard she gave to Sir Accalon.

Then she said to Arthur, "A certain

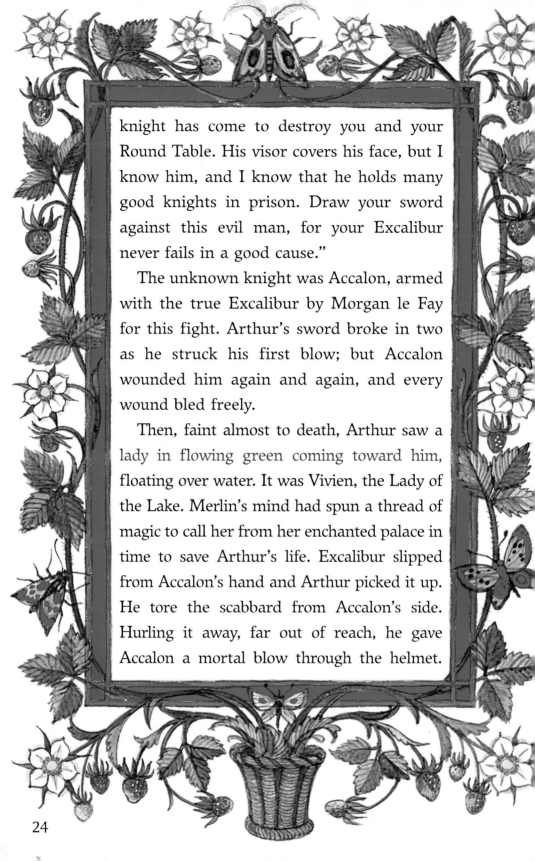

knight has come to destroy you and your Round Table. His visor covers his face, but I know him, and I know that he holds many good knights in prison. Draw your sword against this evil man, for your Excalibur never fails in a good cause."

The unknown knight was Accalon, armed with the true Excalibur by Morgan le Fay for this fight. Arthur's sword broke in two as he struck his first blow; but Accalon wounded him again and again, and every wound bled freely.

Then, faint almost to death, Arthur saw a lady in flowing green coming toward him, floating over water. It was Vivien, the Lady of the Lake. Merlin's mind had spun a thread of magic to call her from her enchanted palace in time to save Arthur's life. Excalibur slipped from Accalon's hand and Arthur picked it up. He tore the scabbard from Accalon's side. Hurling it away, far out of reach, he gave Accalon a mortal blow through the helmet.

Accalon died a few days later, but with the help of Merlin, Arthur's wounds healed quickly. Once again he had Excalibur and the magic scabbard.

Morgan le Fay did not give up her wicked plans. She knew that Arthur slept with his sword at his side. One night she crept into his room and stole the magic scabbard. Away she sped with it and threw it into outer darkness. It was never seen again. From that time on, King Arthur could be killed like any poor soldier.

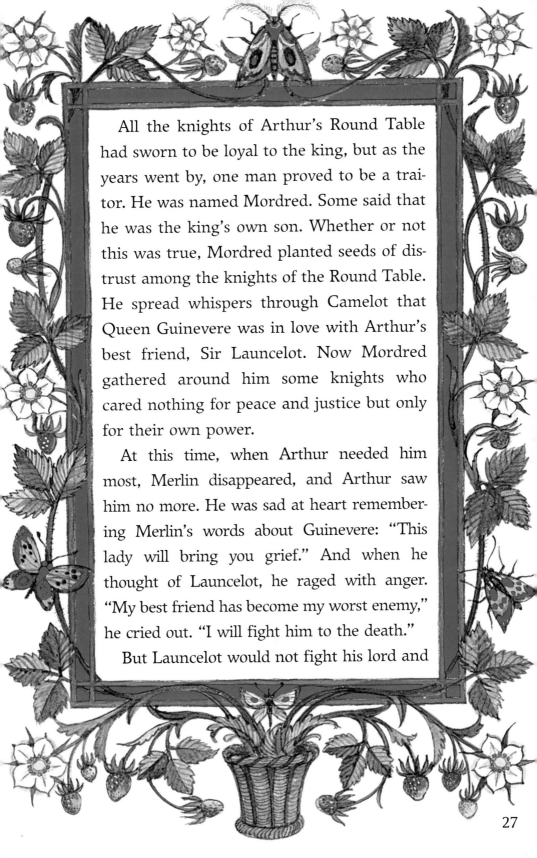

All the knights of Arthur's Round Table had sworn to be loyal to the king, but as the years went by, one man proved to be a traitor. He was named Mordred. Some said that he was the king's own son. Whether or not this was true, Mordred planted seeds of distrust among the knights of the Round Table. He spread whispers through Camelot that Queen Guinevere was in love with Arthur's best friend, Sir Launcelot. Now Mordred gathered around him some knights who cared nothing for peace and justice but only for their own power.

At this time, when Arthur needed him most, Merlin disappeared, and Arthur saw him no more. He was sad at heart remembering Merlin's words about Guinevere: "This lady will bring you grief." And when he thought of Launcelot, he raged with anger. "My best friend has become my worst enemy," he cried out. "I will fight him to the death."

But Launcelot would not fight his lord and

king. He crossed the narrow sea to France, where he had a strong castle and an army of gallant knights. Arthur followed him and besieged Launcelot's castle with his own army, leaving his kingdom in the hands of Mordred, whom he trusted.

THE LADY
OF THE
LAKE

HILE ARTHUR LAID SIEGE to Launcelot's castle in France and demanded that he should come out to fight, word came from England that Mordred had seized the throne and crown for himself. Arthur returned at once and found Mordred's army waiting on the beach to prevent his landing.

Arthur leaped from his flagship with its red dragon banner flying, and all his men poured after him until the air was pierced with shouts

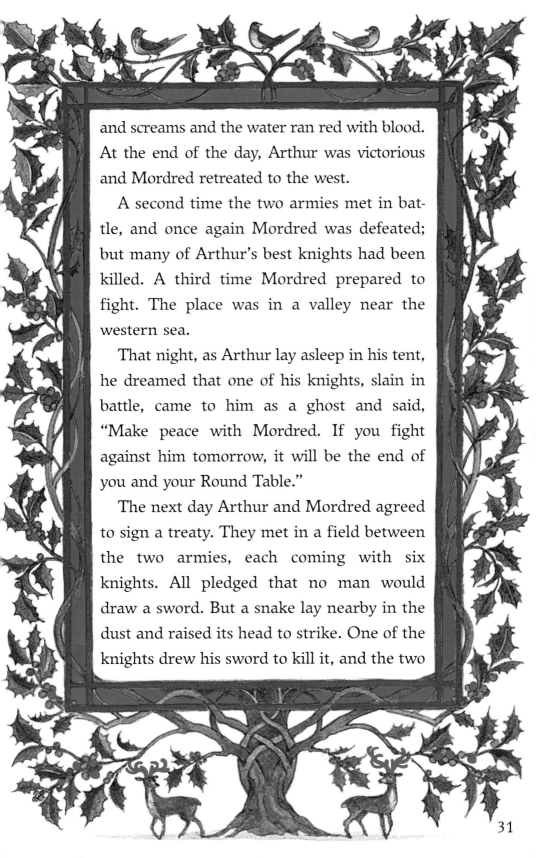

and screams and the water ran red with blood. At the end of the day, Arthur was victorious and Mordred retreated to the west.

A second time the two armies met in battle, and once again Mordred was defeated; but many of Arthur's best knights had been killed. A third time Mordred prepared to fight. The place was in a valley near the western sea.

That night, as Arthur lay asleep in his tent, he dreamed that one of his knights, slain in battle, came to him as a ghost and said, "Make peace with Mordred. If you fight against him tomorrow, it will be the end of you and your Round Table."

The next day Arthur and Mordred agreed to sign a treaty. They met in a field between the two armies, each coming with six knights. All pledged that no man would draw a sword. But a snake lay nearby in the dust and raised its head to strike. One of the knights drew his sword to kill it, and the two

armies saw the blade flash. "Treason!" they shouted, and grimly they rushed to fight.

Thus began Arthur's last great battle, and the sun went up the sky and sank in the west. When night fell, the moon shone down on the battlefield where Arthur stood with a hundred thousand knights lying dead around him. Only one of his friends, Sir Bedivere, remained alive, but another knight

faced Arthur with his sword drawn. It was
Mordred.

Arthur cried, "Traitor, defend yourself!"
and ran toward Mordred, leveling his lance.
Mordred ran straight toward Arthur, his
sword raised in both hands, and the lance
pierced his body. Still he came on, and
before he fell dead, he smote Arthur through
the helmet.

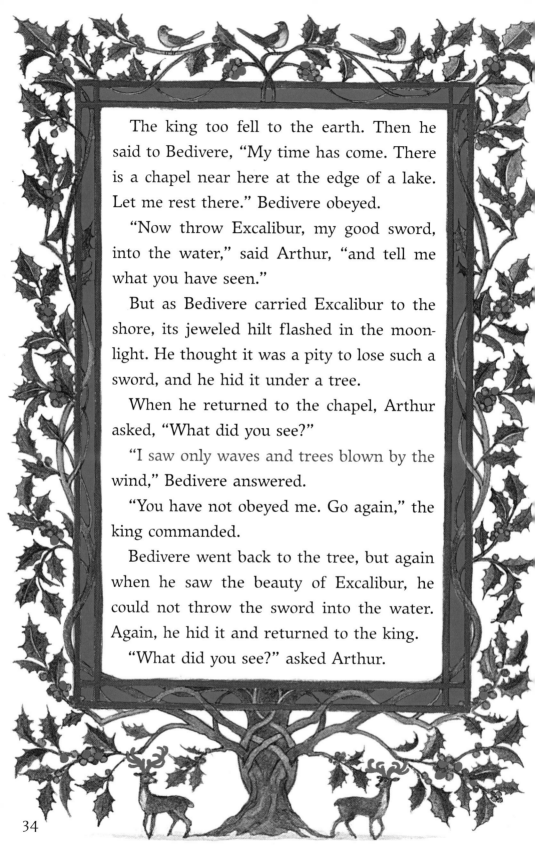

The king too fell to the earth. Then he said to Bedivere, "My time has come. There is a chapel near here at the edge of a lake. Let me rest there." Bedivere obeyed.

"Now throw Excalibur, my good sword, into the water," said Arthur, "and tell me what you have seen."

But as Bedivere carried Excalibur to the shore, its jeweled hilt flashed in the moonlight. He thought it was a pity to lose such a sword, and he hid it under a tree.

When he returned to the chapel, Arthur asked, "What did you see?"

"I saw only waves and trees blown by the wind," Bedivere answered.

"You have not obeyed me. Go again," the king commanded.

Bedivere went back to the tree, but again when he saw the beauty of Excalibur, he could not throw the sword into the water. Again, he hid it and returned to the king.

"What did you see?" asked Arthur.

"The tide is going out," answered Bedivere.

The king's voice reproached him. "I shall die while you delay."

Then Bedivere ran from the chapel and carried the sword to the shore of the lake. He threw it. And as Excalibur flew, glittering in the light of the moon, an arm clothed in shining white rose from the middle of the lake.

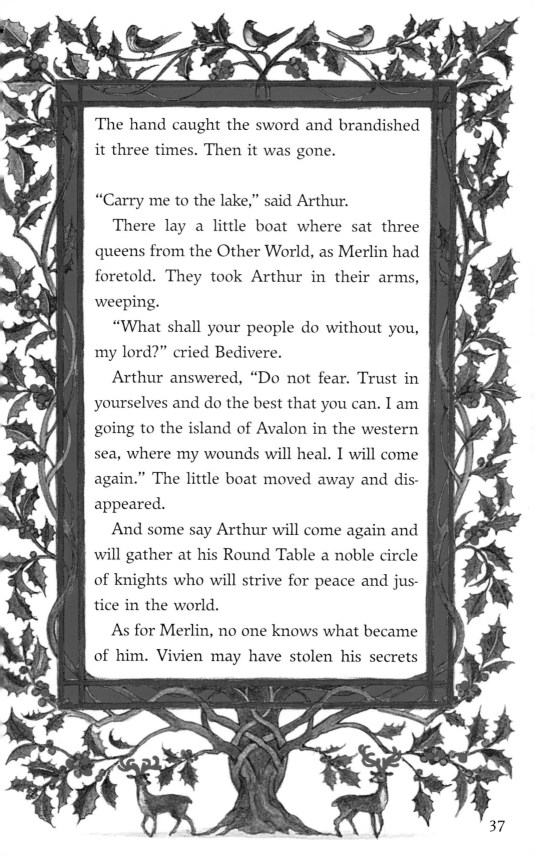

The hand caught the sword and brandished it three times. Then it was gone.

"Carry me to the lake," said Arthur.

There lay a little boat where sat three queens from the Other World, as Merlin had foretold. They took Arthur in their arms, weeping.

"What shall your people do without you, my lord?" cried Bedivere.

Arthur answered, "Do not fear. Trust in yourselves and do the best that you can. I am going to the island of Avalon in the western sea, where my wounds will heal. I will come again." The little boat moved away and disappeared.

And some say Arthur will come again and will gather at his Round Table a noble circle of knights who will strive for peace and justice in the world.

As for Merlin, no one knows what became of him. Vivien may have stolen his secrets and then wrapped him in a spell for sleeping from which he never woke. Some knights spoke of a certain oak tree where they thought Vivien had imprisoned Merlin. They went there for advice and said they could hear him speaking. Others told how they had found a hidden lake and, looking into its clear depths, had seen Merlin walking with Vivien arm in arm through the gardens of an enchanted palace.

No one knows.

AUTHOR'S NOTE

In 1485 *Le Morte d'Arthur*, a manuscript collection of Arthurian legends, was published in London by William Caxton. The author was Sir Thomas Malory, who had identified himself as a "knight prisoner." Like Malory and many others, Caxton believed that Arthur was a real king in the history of early Britain and that in time of need Arthur would come again, "the once and future king." In 1485 this was still the hope and the dream.

Malory had called the city of Winchester "Camelot." In 1934 Dr. W. F. Oakeshott found a manuscript in a library at Winchester College that proved to be closer than the Caxton manuscript to what Malory had actually written. The text here is retold from the Winchester manuscript.

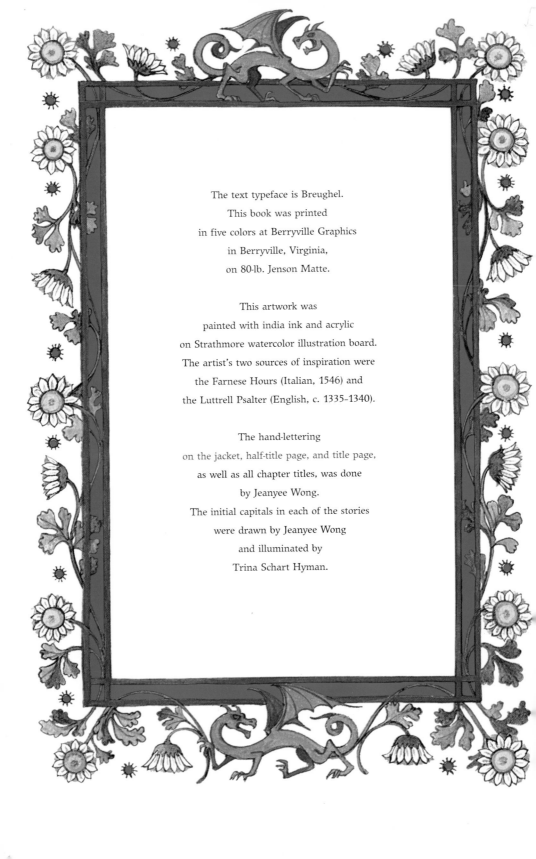

The text typeface is Breughel.
This book was printed
in five colors at Berryville Graphics
in Berryville, Virginia,
on 80-lb. Jenson Matte.

This artwork was
painted with india ink and acrylic
on Strathmore watercolor illustration board.
The artist's two sources of inspiration were
the Farnese Hours (Italian, 1546) and
the Luttrell Psalter (English, c. 1335-1340).

The hand-lettering
on the jacket, half-title page, and title page,
as well as all chapter titles, was done
by Jeanyee Wong.
The initial capitals in each of the stories
were drawn by Jeanyee Wong
and illuminated by
Trina Schart Hyman.